HAMLET

WILLIAM SHAKESPEARE

www.realreads.co.uk

Retold by Helen Street
Illustrated by Charly Cheung

Published by Real Reads Ltd
Stroud, Gloucestershire, UK
www.realreads.co.uk

Text copyright © Helen Street 2012
Illustrations copyright © Charly Cheung 2012
The right of Helen Street to be identified as the
author of this book has been asserted by her in accordance
with the Copyright, Design and Patents Act 1988

ISBN 978-1-906230-55-5

Printed in Singapore by Imago Ltd
Designed by Lucy Guenot
Typeset by Bookcraft Ltd, Stroud, Gloucestershire

CONTENTS

THE CHARACTERS

Hamlet

The Prince of Denmark can't get over the fact that his father died and his mother then married his father's brother. Will his grief and anger lead to something worse?

Claudius and Gertrude, king and queen of Denmark

Now that Claudius has everything – his brother's wife, crown and kingdom – he should be happy. But what is his guilty secret?

Polonius

Polonius is the bumbling busybody advisor to the king. He is keen to solve the mystery of Hamlet's behaviour but will things turn out bad for him?

Laertes and Ophelia

Polonius's son and daughter. Hamlet loves Ophelia and respects Laertes, but his actions turn their worlds upside down.

Horatio

Hamlet's loyal friend. After he tells what he saw one night, all sorts of tragedies unfold. But what was it that he saw?

Rosencrantz and Guildenstern

They are asked to spy on their old school friend, Hamlet. How far will they go to keep the king's favour? As far as England? As far as the gallows?

HAMLET

ACT ONE, SCENE ONE
THE CASTLE AT ELSINORE

Claudius, the new king of Denmark, addresses the royal court.

King

Good friends, though yet of my dear brother's death
The memory be green and it is right to bear our hearts
In grief, yet we must bear remembrance of ourselves,
And so in sorrow and in joy have we our sometime
　　sister wed to be our queen.
But now, my cousin Hamlet, and my son,
How is it that the clouds still hang on you?

Hamlet

Not so, my lord. I am too much in the sun.

Queen

Good Hamlet, cast thy gloomy colour off
And let thine eye look like a friend on Denmark.
Do not forever with thy downcast eye
Seek for thy noble father in the dust.

King

'Tis unmanly grief to grieve so long.
Throw down to earth this woe and think of us

As of a father. For let the world take note,
You are the most immediate to our throne.
And as to your desire to go from here –
We do beseech you to remain at court.

Queen

I pray thee stay with us. Go not to Wittenberg.

Hamlet

I shall in all my best obey you, madam.

King

Why, 'tis a loving and a fair reply.
Be as yourself in Denmark. Madam, come.

All leave except Hamlet.

Hamlet

Oh, that this too too solid flesh would melt,
Thaw, and resolve itself into a dew,
Or that the great almighty had not fixed
His laws against self-slaughter. O god, god,
How weary, stale, flat and unprofitable
Seems to me all the uses of this world!
'Tis but an unweeded garden grown to seed.
That it should come to this! But two months dead –
Before her shoes were old with which she walked
Behind my father's body, my mother

Married with my uncle with wicked speed.
But break, my heart, for I must hold my tongue.

Horatio enters.

Horatio
Hail to your lordship.

Hamlet
Horatio – what brings you here to court?

Horatio
My lord, I came to see your father's funeral.
I saw him once. He was a goodly king.

Hamlet
I shall not look upon his like again.

Horatio
My lord, I think I saw him yesternight.

Hamlet
The king, my father?

Horatio
Aye, my lord, the king.
His ghost, or else his like, was seen to walk
Upon the battlements, but would not speak.

Hamlet
Then I will watch with you tonight. Perhaps
'Twill walk again. If so, I'll challenge it.

ACT ONE, SCENE TWO
A ROOM IN THE CASTLE

Laertes

And now farewell, dear sister, I must leave.

My studies beckon me. I go to France,

But let me hear from you without delay.

Ophelia

Indeed you shall.

Laertes

And as for Hamlet's trifling favour –

Perhaps he loves you now but by his birth,

He is not free to choose the one he wants.

So keep you in the rear of your affection

And wary that you do not lose your heart.

Polonius enters.

Polonius

Yet here, Laertes? Aboard, aboard for shame!

The wind sits in the shoulder of your sail,

But first, my blessing and advice to you.

Those friends thou hast, if they prove true to thee,

Grapple them unto thy soul with hoops
    of steel.

Give every man thy ear, but few thy voice.

Neither a borrower nor a lender be,

For loan oft loses both itself and friend.

This above all: to thine own self be true,

And it must follow, as the night the day,

Thou canst not then be false to any man.

Farewell, my blessings once again to thee.

Laertes

Most humbly do I take my leave, my lord.

Farewell, Ophelia, and remember well

What I have said to you.

Laertes leaves.

Polonius

What is't, Ophelia, he hath said to you?

Ophelia

So please you, something touching the lord Hamlet.

Polonius

What is between you? Give me up the truth.

Ophelia

He hath, my lord, of late, made many tenders

Of his affections to me.

Polonius

Affection, pooh!

Young men say things they do not mean.

From this time forth, have no more talk with him.

Ophelia

I shall obey, my lord.

ACT ONE, SCENE THREE
THE BATTLEMENTS

Hamlet

The air bites shrewdly; it is very cold.
What is the hour?

Horatio

I think 'tis almost twelve.
But look, my lord, it comes!

Ghost appears.

Hamlet

Angels and ministers of grace defend us!
Thou com'st in my father's shape to haunt me,
Say, why is this? Canst thou not rest in peace?

Horatio

It beckons you to go away with it.

Hamlet follows ghost.

Hamlet

Whither wilt thou lead me? Speak, I'll go no
further.

Ghost

If thou didst ever thy dear father love,
Revenge his foul and most unnatural murder.

Hamlet
Murder!

Ghost
'Tis given out that, sleeping in my orchard,
A serpent stung me and 'tis so I died.
The serpent that did sting thy father's life
Now wears his crown.

Hamlet
O, my prophetic soul!
My uncle?

13

Ghost

Into my ear, he poured a poisoned juice.

Thus was I, sleeping, by a brother's hand

Of life, of crown, of queen at once deprived.

Revenge me, Hamlet, and remember me.

Ghost disappears.

Horatio

Heaven preserve thee, my lord, 'tis gone!

Hamlet

Horatio, swear this upon my sword,

Never make known what you have seen tonight.

Horatio

I swear, my lord.

ACT TWO, SCENE ONE
THE CASTLE

Polonius is studying his papers. Ophelia rushes in.

Polonius

How now, Ophelia. What's the matter?

Ophelia

Alas, my lord, I have been so affrighted!

Polonius

With what, in the name of god?

Ophelia

My lord, as I was sewing in my room,
Lord Hamlet, with his clothes in disarray,
Pale as his shirt, his knees knocking each other,
And with a look so piteous to behold
Appeared before me.

Polonius

Mad for thy love?

Ophelia

My lord, I do not know,
But truly I do fear it.

Polonius

This is the very ecstasy of love
That cannot lead to anything of good.
This must be known. I will go seek the king.

ACT TWO, SCENE TWO
THE CASTLE

*Rosencrantz and Guildenstern come before
the king and queen.*

king

Welcome, dear Rosencrantz and Guildenstern!
You answer swift my hasty summons here.

As you are friends from our dear Hamlet's youth,
Perhaps he will reveal to you the cause
Of his most recent transformation –
His strange behaviour, more than grief should show.

Guildenstern

We lay our service freely at your feet.

Queen

And I beseech you instantly to visit
My too much changéd son. Go, find him out.

Rosencrantz and Guildenstern leave. Polonius enters.

Polonius

My lord, I do believe that I have found
The very cause of Hamlet's lunacy.

King

O speak of that: that do I long to hear.

Queen

I doubt it is no other but two things:
His father's death and our o'er hasty marriage.

Polonius

I will be brief. Your noble son is mad –
Is mad with love for fair Ophelia.

King

How shall we know if this is true?

Polonius

I'll bid my daughter wait for him sometime
When he goes pacing up and down this hall,
As is his custom. We will watch concealed
And mark his countenance when they do meet.

Queen

But look where sadly the poor wretch comes reading.

Polonius

Away, I do beseech you both, away!

King, queen and Polonius leave. Hamlet enters alone,
reading. Rosencrantz and Guildenstern enter.

Guildenstern

My honoured lord!

Rosencrantz

My most dear lord!

Hamlet

My excellent good friends!
Good lads, how do you both?

Guildenstern

Happy, in that we are not over-happy,
On Fortune's cap we are not the very button.

Hamlet

What brings you here to Elsinore?

Rosencrantz

To visit you, my lord, no other reason.

Hamlet

Your looks betray you. I know that you were sent for,
  and I will tell you why.
I have of late, but know not why, lost all my mirth
  and indeed, so heavy are my spirits that even
  this good earth seems but a barren land.
This sky, this majestical roof fretted with golden fire,
  appears to me but foul and polluted gas.

A flourish of trumpets.

Rosencrantz

My lord, we passed a band of players on our way,
And here they come to offer service to the court.

Players enter.

Hamlet

Gentlemen, you are welcome to Elsinore.
We'll hear a play tomorrow. Can you play *The
  Murder of Gonzago?*

Player

Aye, my lord.

Hamlet

We'll have that, and I will write some extra lines
for you to say.

(to Rosencrantz and Guildenstern) Now, see these
players well-provided for. Take them in.

All leave except Hamlet.

I'll have these players play something resembling
The murder of my father, before the king.
I'll watch my uncle's face to see if he
Betrays his guilt. Then will I know my task,
When I have proof. Oh yes, the play's the thing
Wherein I'll catch the conscience of the king.

ACT TWO, SCENE THREE
THE CASTLE

King

And did you get from him the very cause
Of his confusion?

Rosencrantz

Answer will he not,
But with a crafty madness keeps aloof.

Guildenstern

Yet with a kind of joy he did receive
The news that certain players were in court.

Polonius

'Tis true. And he beseeched me to request
Your majesties' attendance at the play.

King

With all my heart.
(to Rosencrantz and Guildenstern) Go stay with him a while.

Rosencrantz and Guildenstern leave.

Sweet Gertrude, leave us, too. Hamlet is sent for
That he may meet, as if by accident,
The fair Ophelia.
Polonius and I will watch unseen and judge
If't be the affliction of his love or no
That thus he suffers for.

The queen leaves.

Polonius

Ophelia, walk you here. Read on this book.

I hear him coming; let's withdraw my lord.

*Polonius and the king hide. Hamlet enters but
does not see Ophelia at first.*

Hamlet

To be, or not to be; that is the question:

Whether 'tis better to suffer the pain

That life may bring, or else to end it all.

To die, to sleep, perchance to dream, ah me.

But in that sleep of death, what dreams may come

When we have shuffled off this mortal coil?

But soft, the fair Ophelia!

Ophelia

My lord.

I have some gifts of yours I would return.

Hamlet

I did love you once.

Ophelia

Indeed, my lord, you made me so believe.

Hamlet

You should not have believed me. I loved you not.

I am a man, and all of us are knaves.

Get thee to a nunnery! Why bring into this world
   more sinners?

To a nunnery go, and quickly, too. Farewell.

Hamlet leaves.

Ophelia

O, heavenly powers, restore him. Woe is me,

He is so changed.

King

Love? I do not think that there is love

Behind his madness, good Polonius.

And yet there's something in his soul could prove

Some danger to us all, therefore, shall I

Decree that Hamlet soon be sent away.

Polonius

My lord, do as you please, but if you will,

Allow his mother all alone to talk

To him about his grief.

ACT THREE, SCENE ONE
THE CASTLE

Hamlet

There is a play tonight before the king:
One scene of it comes near the circumstance,
Which I have told thee, of my father's death.
I pray you, when you see that act, observe
My uncle. If he does not show his guilt,
The ghost we saw did not speak fair and true.

Horatio

If he betray the slightest down-cast eye
I'll find him out.

Hamlet

They are coming to the play. Get you a place.

*King, queen and courtiers enter and take their seats. The actors
begin their show in mime. Enter a king and queen who lovingly
embrace. The king lies down on a bed of flowers as if in a garden.
When he falls asleep, the queen leaves him. Another man enters
and takes the crown gently from the sleeping king's head. The
man kisses the crown and pours poison into the king's ear,
then leaves. The queen returns, finds the king dead and weeps
passionately. The other man returns and comforts her. The body
is covered over. The poisoner woos the queen with gifts. She rejects
them at first but then is won over by him. He places the king's
crown on his head and walks off with the queen hand in hand.*

Ophelia

The king rises.

Polonius

Stop the play!

King

Give me some light. Enough!

Polonius

Lights, lights, lights!

> *The king storms out. Everyone leaves except*
> *Horatio and Hamlet.*

Hamlet

O good Horatio, saw you that?

Horatio

Indeed.

Hamlet

The ghost spoke true. There was the proof.

> *Polonius enters.*

Polonius

The king, my lord, is out of sorts!

Hamlet

With drink?

Polonius
No, sir, in anger. I am sent to say
The queen desires to speak to you at once.

Hamlet
Then I will come to my mother by and by.

ACT THREE, SCENE TWO
THE CASTLE

King
I like him not, nor stands it safe with us
To let his madness range. Therefore prepare you,
And he to England shall along with you.

Guildenstern
We shall do as you say, your majesty.

Rosencrantz and Guildenstern leave.

King
My crime cannot be pardoned, this I know.
As Cain was cursed by heaven, so shall I be.
Perhaps a prayer? 'Forgive me my foul murder'?
That cannot be, since I am still possessed
Of those effects for which I did the murder,
My crown, mine own ambition, and my queen.

He kneels to pray. Hamlet enters, unseen by the king, carrying a sword.

Hamlet

I'll kill him now while he does say his prayers –
Yet if I do then he will go to heaven.
'Tis not revenge to send this villain there.

Hamlet leaves.

King *(rising)*

My words fly up, my thoughts remain below.
Words without thoughts never to heaven go.

ACT THREE, SCENE THREE
THE QUEEN'S BEDROOM

Hamlet *(from outside)*
Mother, mother, mother!

Polonius
Mind well you tell him he has gone too far.
I'll hide behind this curtain and hear all.

Polonius hides and Hamlet enters.

Hamlet
Now, mother, what's the matter?

Queen
Hamlet, thou hast thy father much offended.

Hamlet
Mother, you have my father much offended.

Queen
Have you forgotten who I am?

Hamlet
You are the queen, your husband's brother's wife,
And – would it were not so – you are my mother.

Hamlet grabs the queen's arm.

Queen
Help, help!

Polonius *(behind the curtain)*
Help, help!

Hamlet
What have we here? A rat?

> *Hamlet thrusts his sword through the curtain and Polonius falls dead.*

Queen
O what a rash and bloody deed is this!

Hamlet
A bloody deed! Almost as bad, good mother,
As kill a king and marry with his brother.

Queen
As kill a king!

Hamlet

Ay, lady, 'twas my word.

Your husband is a murderer and a villain.

Queen

O Hamlet, speak no more.

These words like daggers enter in my ears.

Hamlet

You must not tell the king I told you this.

As for this lord, I do repent my deed.

I will answer well the death I gave him –

I must to England, you know that?

Queen

Alack, I had forgot.

Hamlet

There's letters sealed, and my two school-fellows –

Whom I will trust as I will adders fanged –

Will carry them – and me – across the sea.

Mother, good night.

Hamlet leaves, dragging Polonius's body with him.
The king enters.

Queen

Ah, mine own lord, what have I seen tonight!

King

What, Gertrude? How does Hamlet?

Queen

Mad as the sea and wind when both contend
Which is the mightier. He heard a sound
And drawing out his sword he killed unseen
The good Polonius.

King

Oh, heavy deed!
Had I been there in place of that old man,
It would be me who lies now cold and dead.
The sun no sooner shall the mountains touch,
But we will ship him hence. Ho! Guildenstern!

Rosencrantz and Guildenstern enter.

King

Hamlet in madness hath Polonius slain.
Go seek him out. I pray you haste in this.

Rosencrantz and Guildenstern leave.

Come, Gertrude. O come away
My soul is full of discord and dismay.

The king and queen leave.

ACT THREE, SCENE FOUR
A HALL IN THE CASTLE

Rosencrantz

Where he has hidden the dead body, lord,
We cannot get from him.

King

But where is he?

Rosencrantz

Ho, Guildenstern! Bring in my lord.

Guildenstern and Hamlet enter.

King

Now, Hamlet, where's Polonius?

Hamlet

At supper.

King

At supper? Where?

Hamlet

Not where he eats, but where he is eaten –
  by the worm.

King

Where is Polonius?

Hamlet

If you find him not within a month, you will
  smell him as you go up the stairs into the lobby.

King (to attendants)
Go seek him there.

Hamlet
He will stay till you come.

King
We dearly grieve for that which thou hast done
And therefore, we must send thee hence with speed
To England. You must take your leave tonight.

Hamlet leaves with Rosencrantz and Guildenstern.

The letters that they take demand in short
The certain death of Hamlet. Do it, England,
For till I know 'tis done, I'll have no peace.

ACT FOUR, SCENE ONE
A ROOM IN THE CASTLE

Queen
I will not speak with her.

Horatio
Madam, her mood requires your pity now.
She speaks much of her father though her words
Make little sense. She sighs and beats her heart.
'Twere good that she were spoken with.

Ophelia enters, looking and acting strangely.

Ophelia
Where is the beauteous Majesty of Denmark?

Queen
How now, Ophelia?

Ophelia *(singing)*
He is dead and gone, lady,
He is dead and gone;
At his head a grass-green turf,
At his heels a stone.

The king enters.

king
How do you, pretty lady?

Ophelia
They say the owl was a baker's daughter.
Lord, we know what we are,
but know not what we may be.

35

king
How long has she been thus?

Ophelia
I hope all will be well. Come, my coach.
Good night, ladies, good night.

Ophelia leaves.

king *(to Horatio)*
Follow her, Horatio, and keep good watch.
O, this is the poison of deep grief; it springs
All from her father's death – and now behold!
O Gertrude, Gertrude,
When sorrows come, they come not all alone
But in battalions.

Laertes bursts into the room.

Laertes
O thou vile king. Where is my father?

king
Dead.

Queen
But not by him.

Laertes

How came he dead? I'll not be juggled with.

I'll be revenged for what has happened here.

King

That I am guiltless of your father's death,

I do assure you.

Ophelia comes in again holding wild flowers.

Laertes

Dear maid, kind sister, sweet Ophelia!

O heavens, is't possible a young maid's wits

Should be as mortal as an old man's life?

Ophelia

They bore him barefaced on the bier,

Hey non nonny, nonny, hey nonny,

And in his grave rained many a tear –

Fare you well, my dove!

Laertes

By heaven, thy madness shall be paid in full!

Ophelia leaves.

King

I pray thee, calm thyself, good Laertes,

And I will answer all that you would know.

ACT FOUR, SCENE TWO
THE CASTLE

Horatio enters holding an opened letter.

Horatio *(reading)*

'Horatio, we were two days at sea when a pirate
ship gave chase. We, being slow of sail, did
the best we could when they came alongside.
In the fighting I jumped onto their ship,
and as soon as they drew clear of our boat,
I found myself their only prisoner. But they
have treated me well and brought me back to
Denmark's shores in return for favours that I
may give. Come to me with as much haste as
thou wouldst fly death. I have words to speak
in thine ear will make thee dumb. The sailors
that brought this letter will bring thee where I
am. Rosencrantz and Guildenstern hold their
course for England; of them I have much to
tell thee. Farewell, thine own Hamlet.'

ACT FOUR, SCENE THREE
THE CASTLE

King
Now you have heard how blameless I have been,
How Hamlet hath your noble father slain,
So you must put me in your heart for friend.

Laertes
Indeed. Yet still he is at liberty.
Why have you not brought judgement on this man?

King

The queen, his mother, loves her son so much,

That it would break her heart, and so break mine

To see her in distress. And you must know:

So deeply does he hold the people's love,

That they would turn against me if I did.

Laertes

And so I have a noble father lost,

And sister driven mad by loss and grief.

But my revenge will come.

King

It will be so.

Messenger enters with letters.

Messenger

Letters, my lord, from Hamlet.

King

From Hamlet? Who brought them?

Messenger

Sailors, my lord.

Messenger leaves.

King *(reading)*

'High and mighty, you should know that I am in your kingdom. Tomorrow I shall come before you and recount the reason for my sudden return. Hamlet.'

What should this mean? Are all the rest come back?

Laertes

I do not know, my lord, but let him come!
It warms the very sickness in my heart
That I shall live and tell him to his teeth
'Thus diest thou'.

King

If it be so, will you be ruled by me?

Laertes

Ay, my lord.

King

I have a plan. 'Twill make his death appear
An accident and you shall be its source.

Laertes

How shall this be?

King

Your reputation as a skilful swordsman
Has in the past made Hamlet envious
And beg some day to play a match with you.
We'll organise a wager on your skills
And in his great excitement, he will not
Observe that you will use an untipped sword.
So may you stab him for your father's sake.

Laertes

And for the purpose, I'll anoint my sword
With deadly poison to bring certain death.

King

But if you fail to strike him, there must be
Another plan. I'll have prepared for him
A poisoned draught that I will offer him
When he is hot and dry and calls for drink.

The queen enters, distressed.

Queen

One woe doth tread upon another's heel,
So fast they follow. Your sister's drowned, Laertes.

Laertes

Drowned? O where?

Queen

There is a willow grows aslant a brook
And there Ophelia did fantastic garlands make
Of crow-flowers, nettles, daisies, and long-purples.
But clamb'ring on the bough to hang them there,
It broke, and she fell in the weeping brook.
Her clothes spread wide and bore her up awhile
Till that her garments, heavy with their drink
Pulled down the poor wretch to a muddy death.

Laertes

Alas, then she is drowned?

Too much of water hast thou, poor Ophelia,

And therefore I forbid my tears.

Laertes leaves.

King

Let's follow, Gertrude.

How much I had to do to calm his rage!

Now fear I this will start it all again.

43

ACT FIVE, SCENE ONE
THE GRAVEYARD

Horatio and Hamlet enter. A gravedigger is digging a grave and singing.

Hamlet

Has this fellow no feeling of his business,
   that he sings at grave-making?

Horatio

He is used to it, my lord.

Hamlet *(to gravedigger)*

How long hast thou been a gravemaker?

Gravedigger

I came to it that very day that young Hamlet was
   born, he that is mad and sent into England.

Hamlet

Why was he sent into England?

Gravedigger

Why, because he was mad. He shall recover
   his wits there, and if he do not, it's no great
   matter there.

Hamlet

Why?

Gravedigger

No one will notice it, for there the men are as mad
as he!

Hamlet

Whose skull is that?

Gravedigger

He was a mad rogue. He poured a flagon of wine
over my head once. This same skull, sir, was
Yorick's skull, the king's jester.

Hamlet *(holding the skull)*

Alas, poor Yorick. I knew him, Horatio,
a fellow of infinite jest.

He hath borne me on his back a thousand times.

Here hung those lips that I have kissed I know
not how oft.

Yet here is all that's left of man – some bones
and dust.

A funeral procession enters, led by Laertes,
the king and queen.

But soft! Let's step aside. Here comes the king,
The queen, the courtiers. Who is that they follow?

Laertes

Oh, lay her in the earth and from this place
    May violets spring.

A heavenly angel shall my sister be.

Queen *(scattering flowers)*

Sweets to the sweet. Farewell.

I hoped thou shouldst have been my
    Hamlet's wife.

Hamlet *(to Horatio)*

What, the fair Ophelia?

Laertes

And cursed be he that was the cause of this.

Hamlet comes towards the coffin.

Hamlet

Now shall I, Hamlet the Dane, show my grief.

Laertes *(seizing Hamlet by the throat)*

The devil take thy soul!

Hamlet

I prithee take thy fingers from my throat.

Attendants part them.

I loved Ophelia. Forty thousand brothers
Could not with all their quantity of love
Make up my sum!

King
Pluck them asunder.

Queen
Hamlet, Hamlet!

King
Oh, he is mad, Laertes.

Hamlet *(to Laertes)*
I know not why you treat me as you do.

Hamlet leaves.

King
I pray thee, good Horatio, attend your lord.

Horatio follows Hamlet.

King *(aside to Laertes)*
Patience, my friend. Our plan will soon succeed.

ACT FIVE, SCENE TWO
THE GREAT HALL OF THE CASTLE

Hamlet

As I did tell you, good Horatio,
I had misgivings of young Rosencrantz
And of young Guildenstern, my one-time friends.
So, on the voyage, while they were fast asleep
I read the letters from the king. In short,
They ordered that my head should be struck off.

Horatio

'Tis hard to believe it, my lord.

A courtier enters.

Courtier

My lord, his Majesty has bid me tell you that he has
laid a wager on your head. He has bet six horses
against six French swords that you will beat
Laertes at fencing by at least three hits.

Hamlet

I am sorry I behaved so badly to Laertes. But I shall
put that right and join him in this friendly match.
Let the foils be brought.

Horatio

You will lose this wager, my lord.

Hamlet

I do not think so. Since he went to France, I have
  been in continual practice.

And yet there is an ill feeling in my heart.

Horatio

If thy mind dislike anything, obey it.

I will stall them and say you are not fit.

Hamlet

No, I will defy these warnings.

If it is my time to die, then let it be.

Who can tell what future waits for us?

The readiness is all.

Laertes, king, queen and attendants enter.

Hamlet *(to Laertes)*

Give me your pardon, sir. I have done you wrong.

What I have done, I here proclaim was madness.

Laertes

I cannot offer pardon at this time

Yet will I be a gentleman in this.

Hamlet

Thanks be for that. Now come, give us the foils.

Foils are brought for Hamlet and Laertes to choose.
Attendants bring goblets of wine to set before the
king and queen.

King

You know the wager?

Hamlet

Very well, my lord.

King

Set me the cups of wine upon that table.

If Hamlet give the first or second hit,

The king shall drink to Hamlet's better skill.

Come, sirs, begin!

Hamlet and Laertes fence. Hamlet scores a hit.

King

Stay, give me drink. Hamlet, this pearl is thine.

Here's to thy health! *(puts pearl into cup)*

Give him the cup!

Hamlet

I'll play this bout first; set it by a while.

Hamlet scores a second hit.
The queen picks up the cup of wine.

Queen

The queen shall drink to thy fortune, Hamlet.

She drinks.

King

Gertrude, do not drink.

Queen
I will, my lord; I pray you, pardon me.

King *(aside)*
It is the poisoned cup – it is too late!

Hamlet
I dare not drink yet, madam; by and by.
Come, for the third, Laertes. You do but dally.
The third bout begins and Laertes wounds Hamlet with his foil.
In the scuffle, the foils are mixed up. The queen falls down.

Attendant
Look to the queen there, ho!

Hamlet wounds Laertes with the poisoned sword.

Horatio
They bleed on both sides! How is it, my lord?

Laertes
I am justly killed with mine own treachery.

Hamlet
How does the queen?

King
She swoons to see them bleed.

Queen
No, no, the drink, the drink! O my dear Hamlet!
The drink, the drink! I am poisoned! *(She dies)*

Hamlet

O villainy! Ho! Let the door be locked.
Treachery! Seek it out.

Laertes

It is here, Hamlet. Hamlet, thou art slain.
No med'cine in the world can do you good.
In thee there is not half an hour's life.
The treacherous instrument is in thy hand,
Untipped and laced with venom.
'Tis the king –
The king's to blame.

Hamlet

The point envenomed too!
Then, venom, do thy work.

Hamlet stabs the king.

King

O, yet defend me, friends: I am but hurt.

Hamlet

Then drink this potion, murderous Dane!

Hamlet makes the king drink from the poisoned cup.
The king dies.

Laertes

Exchange forgiveness with me, noble Hamlet:
Mine and my father's death come not upon thee,
Nor thine on me. *(dies)*

Hamlet

Heaven make thee free of it! I follow thee.
I am dead, Horatio.
If thou didst ever hold me in thy heart,
Live after me that you, with painful breath,
May tell my story. *(dies)*

Horatio

Now cracks a noble heart. Good night, sweet prince,
And flights of angels sing thee to thy rest.

TAKING THINGS FURTHER

The real read

This *Real Reads* version of *Hamlet* is a retelling of William Shakespeare's magnificent work. If you would like to read the full play in all its original splendour, many complete editions are available, from bargain paperbacks to beautifully-bound hardbacks. You may well find a copy in your local charity shop.

Filling in the spaces

The loss of so many of William Shakespeare's original words is a sad but necessary part of the shortening process. We have had to make some difficult decisions, omitting subplots and details, some important, some less so, but all interesting. We have also, at times, taken the liberty of combining two events into one, or of giving a character words or actions that originally belong to another. The points below will fill in some of the gaps, but nothing can beat the original.

- The play opens with soldiers discussing the threatened war with Norway, led by Fortinbras, the nephew of the King of Norway.

- In several scenes, Hamlet teases Polonius and other courtiers, confirming their opinion that he is mad.

- When the players arrive, Hamlet gives them advice on how to perform their speeches – just as Shakespeare himself might have done with his own actors.

- Hamlet makes several long speeches where he considers the meaning of life and of what might come after death. These are known as his great soliloquies.

- On board ship to England, Hamlet secretly rewrites the orders Rosencrantz and Guildenstern carry to England, so that his former friends will be executed instead of him.

- The gravediggers discuss whether Ophelia was drowned or committed suicide.

- At the end, Fortinbras arrives after victory over Poland and claims the throne of Denmark with Hamlet's dying blessing.

Back in time

William Shakespeare was born in 1564 in Stratford on Avon, and later went to London where he became an actor and playwright. He was very popular in his own lifetime. He wrote thirty-seven plays that we know of, and many sonnets.

The very first theatres were built around the time that Shakespeare was growing up. Until then, plays were performed in rooms at the back of inns, or pubs. The Elizabethans loved going to watch entertainments such as bear-baiting and cock-fighting as well as plays. They also liked to watch public executions, and some of the plays written at this time were quite gruesome.

The Globe, where Shakespeare's company acted, was a round wooden building that was open to the sky in the middle. 'Groundlings' paid a penny to stand around the stage in the central yard. They risked getting wet if it rained. Wealthier people could have a seat in the covered galleries around the edge of the space. Some very important people even had a seat on the stage itself. Unlike today's theatre-goers, Elizabethan audiences were noisy and sometimes fighting broke out.

There were no sets or scene changes in these plays. It was up to the playwright's skill with words to create thunderstorms or forests or Egyptian queens in the imagination of the audience.

Shakespeare wrote mostly in blank verse, in unrhymed lines of ten syllables with a te-tum te-tum rhythm. But unlike most writers of his time, he tried to make his actors' lines closer to the rhythms of everyday speech, in order to make it sound more naturalistic. He used poetic imagery, and even invented words that we still use today.

His plays are mostly based on stories or old plays that he improved. *Hamlet* is a reworking

of an earlier play from Elizabethan times, but
the story can be traced to a twelfth-century true
story of Amleth whose uncle, Feng, murdered
Amleth's father and married his mother.

Finding out more

We recommend the following books and
websites to gain a greater understanding
of William Shakespeare and Elizabethan
England.

Books

- Marcia Williams, *Mr William Shakespeare's
Plays*, Walker Books, 2009.

- Leon Garfield, *Shakespeare Stories*, Victor
Gollanz, 1985.

- Stewart Ross, *William Shakespeare: Writers
in Britain series*, Evans, 1999.

- Felicity Hebditch, *Tudors, Britain through
the Ages series*, Evans, 2003.

- Dereen Taylor, *The Tudors and the Stuarts*,
Wayland, 2007.

Websites

- www.shakespeare.org.uk
Good general introduction to the life of Shakespeare. Contains information and pictures of the houses linked to him in and around Stratford.

- www.elizabethan-era.org.uk
Lots of information including details of Elizabethan daily life

- www.sparknotes.com/shakespeare
See the original texts side by side with a modern English translation.

Films

- *Shakespeare: The Animated Tales*, 2007, DVD Metrodome Distribution Ltd.

- *Hamlet*, 1996. PG 12. Castle Rock Entertainments, directed by and starring Kenneth Branagh.

- *Hamlet*, 2009. PG 12. BBC, directed by Gregory Doran, starring David Tennant.

Food for thought

Here are some things to think about if you are reading *Hamlet* alone, or ideas for discussion if you are reading it with friends.

In retelling *Hamlet* we have tried to recreate, as accurately as possible, Shakespeare's original plot and characters. We have also tried to imitate aspects of his style. Remember, however, that this is not the original work; thinking about the points below, therefore, can help you begin to understand William Shakespeare's craft. To move forward from here, turn to the full-length version of *Hamlet* and lose yourself in his wonderful storytelling.

Starting points

● Why does Hamlet hesitate to tell everyone that Claudius is a murderer?

● Why do you think Ophelia goes mad?

● Why does Claudius send Hamlet away to England?

- Do you think Hamlet was really mad or was he pretending? Why would he pretend?

Themes

What do you think William Shakespeare is saying about the following themes in *Hamlet*?

- revenge
- family relationships
- grief

Style

Can you find examples of the following?

- a character speaking in prose
- a character speaking in blank verse
- poetic imagery
- a soliloquy – a speech spoken when the character is alone

Try your hand at writing an iambic pentameter. It must have ten syllables arranged in pairs; the first syllable of each pair is unstressed and the second is stressed, like this from *Hamlet*:

How *is* it *that* the *clouds* still *hang* on *you*?

Something old, something new

In this *Real Reads* version of *Hamlet*, Shakespeare's original words have been interwoven with new linking text in Shakespearean style. If you are interested in knowing which words are original and which new, visit www.realreads.co.uk/shakespeare/ comparison/hamlet – here you will find a version with the original words highlighted. It might be fun to guess in advance which are which!

CAST LIST

Major speaking roles

Hamlet, Prince of Denmark
Claudius, Hamlet's uncle
Gertrude, Hamlet's mother
Polonius, advisor to the king
Laertes, Polonius's son

Minor speaking roles

Ghost
Ophelia, Polonius's daughter
Horatio, friend to Hamlet
Rosencrantz, Hamlet's old schoolfriend
Guildenstern, Hamlet's old schoolfriend
Gravedigger

One-liners

Courtier/Messenger/Attendant

Non-speaking roles

Players
Courtiers
Servants